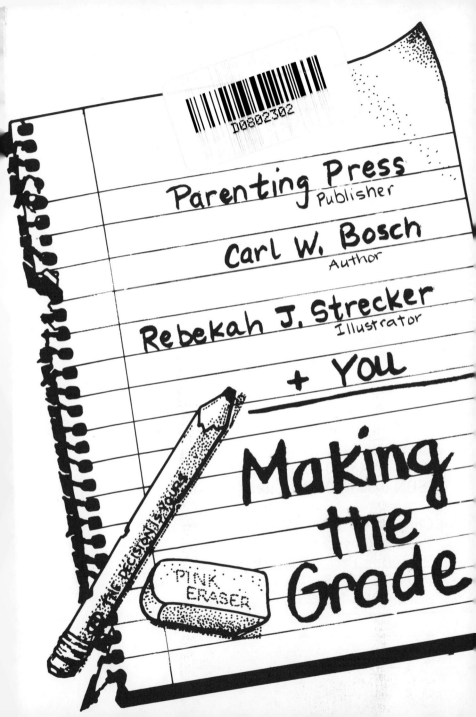

Parenting Press
Publisher

Carl W. Bosch
Author

Rebekah J. Strecker
Illustrator

+ You

Making
the
Grade

PINK
ERASER

LC 90-62674
ISBN 0-943990-48-3 Paper
ISBN 0-943990-49-1 Library Binding

Copyright © 1991, Parenting Press, Inc.
Published by:
Parenting Press, Inc.
P.O. Box 75267
Seattle, WA 98125

BEFORE YOU BEGIN

Most books you read tell you about other people's decisions.

This book is different! *You* make the decisions. *You* decide what happens next.

Have you ever made a decision and found things didn't turn out the way you planned? It happens all the time. Did you ever dream about going back and trying again? What would have happened if you had done something differently?

In this book you'll find out how it feels when you get a bad report card. You'll have lots of chances to choose different ways of acting. You make the decisions. Good luck!

Turn the page and see what happens.

1

The first term of fourth grade has just finished, **2** and it's report card day. You've been awfully busy this fall. Last week your soccer team won the championship for your division, and you scored the winning goal!

You spent a lot of time during September and October practicing with the team. You had to make your Halloween costume and that took two weeks. You really haven't been paying attention to homework, studying, and tests.

Ms. Shelton, your teacher, hands you your report card and says, "Jennifer, playtime is over; you'd better get to work this term!"

When you look at your report card, you can't believe it. All you see are two C's, two D's and an F. The worst you ever did before was a C- when you were in the school play and had to practice every night. Your eyes start to fill up, and a tear drops on the desk in front of you.

What are your parents going to say?

Turn to page 4.

Your heart is racing. This is the worst report **4** card you have ever received. Quickly, you look around the room to see if your friends have noticed you.

Only Karen, who sits two seats across, is looking at you. Karen wiggles her ears and makes a crazy face. She's always doing that. She smiles, but as soon as she sees your face, she looks worried.

You look away and fold up your report card, shoving it into your pocket. You try to figure out what you're going to do. Suddenly, you think about not showing your parents at all. At least not until the big soccer tournament is over this weekend. The soccer tournament is important; last year the Strikers beat your team, the Lions. You really want to win this game. You're thinking about it when the bell rings.

*If you are not going to tell your parents,
turn to page 6.*

If you're not sure what to do, turn to page 7.

As you walk out the door, you make up your mind **6** not to tell your parents. You know that they will probably find out sometime, but you are not going to help them. If they see those D's and that F, they might not let you play in the tournament.

Karen catches up with you and makes another goofy face. "How did you do?" she asks.

"Please, don't even ask," you answer.

"Don't worry, I'll visit you in the dungeon," she jokes.

"It isn't funny," you reply. Karen realizes you're not laughing.

"That bad, huh?" she asks.

"A total disaster," you declare, "but I have a solution. I'm not showing my parents."

"Are you serious?" she exclaims.

If you decide to talk to Karen more, turn to page 10.

If you are sure you're not showing your parents, turn to page 12.

7   You walk out into the hall, and Karen catches up with you.

"That bad?" she asks. Karen is your best friend. She plays striker on your soccer team and can run faster than almost anyone in the fourth grade. She loves pizza, swimming, and movies. And she does well in school. But most of all, she is funny.

You shake your head, and you can feel the lump in your throat again.

"What am I going to do?" you ask. "My parents will ground me, or worse."

"There are lots of things you can do!" she exclaims.

"Like what?" you look at her.

"We can run away and become professional soccer players. Pele, watch out!" she laughs.

"Karen, come on!" you say miserably. She hears the worried sound in your voice.

"Okay, okay. Well, for starters, you could go talk to Ms. Shelton," she says honestly.

If you don't want to talk to Ms. Shelton,
turn to page 13.

If you decide to talk with Ms. Shelton,
turn to page 16.

As you walk home, you and Karen talk about the **10** problem.

"I just can't get that dumb math," you complain. "And those spelling tests are so hard!"

"Look, you're not dumb," Karen pointed out. "It's just that you've been busy and not paying much attention to your homework. You're always playing soccer with us and your brothers. Look how good you are now. You are the best forward in the league."

"Once my parents find out, I'm the best ex-forward, you mean," you say glumly.

Karen ignores your joke and goes on.

"Here's my idea. I'll be your tutor. We can stay after school every day for an hour. We'll study together, and I'll help with the real hard homework. We'll work hard for tests. You can ask your parents to give you one more chance.

"If it doesn't work, tell them you'll stay in your room until you're eighteen!" she finished.

You smile for the first time that afternoon. Karen turns down her street and waves.

"But what if it doesn't work?" you call to her.

"Come on! What does coach always say? 'Lions, Lions! Don't stop try-in'!'" she calls back.

Turn to page 18.

That evening at home you are scared. Luckily, **12** your brothers go to the high school and have a different schedule. Their report cards don't come out until next week. Somehow, your parents just forget to ask about your report card.

"Jen!" your dad laughs as you jump out of your chair. He gives you a hug. "I only said hello."

Before bedtime, your brother Dan, who is a junior and an all-county soccer player, stops you in the kitchen. "Jen, you're acting weird tonight. Hey, didn't report cards come out today at your school?" he asks.

He can tell by the look on your face that they did.

"Come on, let's take a look at it," he says.

In a few minutes, you've told him the entire story and shown him the report card.

"Listen, I think you ought to tell Mom and Dad," he says. "If you talk to them in a mature way, they'll understand. Or how about if I help you? They don't call me a math wizard for nothing. I'll teach you the multiplication tables so you'll never forget them."

You look at your cat, Skimble, who's trying to steal Dan's sandwich. Then you look at Dan, trying to decide.

If you decide to tell your parents, turn to page 20.

If you want Dan to help you, turn to page 21.

If you don't want any help at all, turn to page 30.

13   "No way!" you exclaim to Karen. "There is no way I can talk to Ms. Shelton. She's the one who's giving me the bad grades!"

"Well, not exactly," Karen answers.

"What do you mean?" you ask.

"You're the one who gets the grades, not Ms. Shelton," she says. Then she gives you another crazy look and heads out the door.

Your parents forget to ask you about the report card that night. They go to the health club to do aerobics and lift weights.

The next day during the social studies test you feel worried. You don't know most of the answers.

You sit next to Josh Harkins, who is the brain of the fourth grade. Josh doesn't cover his paper very well, and you can easily see all the answers to the multiple choice questions.

According to Josh's paper, the capital of Vermont is Montpelier. You had it wrong! You've never cheated before, but here is your golden chance for a good grade.

You take another look around the room. No one is looking at you. You take another peek at Josh's paper....

If you decide to cheat, turn to page 23.

If you decide not to cheat, turn to page 24.

You think for a minute and realize that Karen **16** usually gives you good advice.

"I'm afraid to talk to Ms. Shelton," you admit.

"I guarantee you she won't bite your head off," says Karen. "She had a big lunch today."

You laugh, turn around, and head back toward the classroom. At the doorway to the classroom, you take a deep breath and walk inside. Ms. Shelton can be really nice, but sometimes she can also be scary.

"Ms. Shelton, can I talk with you for a minute?" you ask.

She looks up from feeding the hamsters. You look at the brown paper bag she is holding and remember what Karen said about Ms. Shelton's lunch.

"What is it, Jennifer?" she asks.

"I got a terrible report card. I'm afraid to take it home, and I don't know what to do," you say. Your voice is almost shaking.

Ms. Shelton looks at you for a long time.

"Jennifer, I can help you, if you're willing to work. School or sports, it's all the same: work produces results! Are you willing to work with me?"

If you are willing to work with Ms. Shelton, turn to page 26.

If you really don't want to work, turn to page 28.

You decide to take Karen up on her idea. You go to your parents, who are in the kitchen planning to go spelunking; they just love to explore caves.

You turn over the report card and tell them what you'd like to do. To your suprise, they agree to give you a chance. They say you can still play sports as long as your grades improve.

The next two months are the hardest you can remember. The very next weekend your team beats the Strikers 3 to 1. In the championship game against Middletown Magic, you score the winning goal! You also try out for and make the basketball team.

But while all this is happening, you also work with Karen *every* day and sometimes even on weekends. You do every bit of your homework. You also work hard on your social studies report on Benjamin Franklin and one for science on the honey bee.

It's hard, but it's fun to work with Karen. You know you're doing better.

Turn to page 32.

You think about it and decide that there is no way around it, you're going to have to tell your parents. Walking into the family room, you say, "I got my report card today."

They can tell by the tone of your voice that something is wrong. Skimble looks up at you sympathetically and then goes back to sleep. You hand the report card over.

Your dad studies it for a long time. He tugs at his chin which usually means he's pretty mad. But all he says is, "Your mom and I are going to have to talk this over. We'll talk to you about it in the morning."

At breakfast your parents meet you at the kitchen table. Your dad is still tugging his chin. Your mom looks stern too.

"Jennifer," she says, "you have two choices. You can sign up for a study skills course at the tutoring school; or we are going to monitor your homework, studying, and grades. The choice is up to you."

Since it's the end of the soccer season, they are going to let you finish the year. They say making you quit wouldn't be fair to the rest of the team.

"But you are not trying out for basketball, young lady," your dad says.

If you choose the study skills course, turn to page 34.

If you choose to have your parents monitor your work, turn to page 36.

21　　You agree to work with Dan. He turns out to be a pretty good teacher. Each night, for about an hour, you work with him. He goes over your math homework and quizzes you on spelling words. For the first couple of weeks, you feel like you are really improving.

Then your coach calls a special evening soccer practice, so you can't study with Dan. You also go to a sleepover at Karen's one night. Your effort begins to fall off. You've been thinking about the holidays and all kinds of other things. Dan is busy on his soccer team, but he still works with you.

One night he sits you down and says, "Jen, you have to decide if you really want to get better grades or not. For awhile it was working fine, but only when you were putting in the effort. Look at this last English test and this Math quiz. You can do better. What's it going to be?"

You feel grumpy, even though you know Dan is right.

"Don't I ever get to have any fun?" you exclaim.

*If you listen to Dan and really work hard,
turn to page 38.*

If you just can't put the effort in, turn to page 40.

23   It's really pretty easy to cheat. You could see all Josh's multiple choice answers without any trouble. The fill-ins are pretty easy, too. Your heart beats fast the entire time.

You take a quick look at Ms. Shelton to see if she's looking at you. She's talking with another student.

Even after the test, you are nervous. That day as you are walking home you get to thinking about cheating and whether you should do it or not. Ms. Shelton is a tough grader. And it's not like you aren't trying.

The next day you receive the paper back with a B+ at the top. You can't believe it! On your last test, you got a D. You wonder if Ms. Shelton is suspicious.

Cheating is scary, and you are really afraid of getting caught.

If you decide to cheat again, turn to page 41.

If you decide never to cheat again, turn to page 58.

It feels like Josh's paper is calling you, and you 24
almost do cheat. But then something inside you
says, "No, it's not right. Besides, I might get
caught." You look away and work on your own
test, which is hard enough.

The questions on the social studies test are hard.
You can't remember all the state capitals.

Walking home, you feel strange, kind of proud
and kind of dumb all at the same time. You walk in
the house. Your mom is putting some batteries in
the camping flashlights. You aren't sure why, but
you suddenly feel brave.

"Mom, I need to talk to you," you take a deep
breath. "I got my report card, and it's really bad.
I was even going to cheat off another kid's test
today, but I just couldn't. Here it is."

Your mom takes the report card. She frowns
when she reads it, but then, suprisingly, she sighs
and gives you a big hug.

"This report card is important," she says, "and
we're going to work at getting those grades up. But
even more important is the decision you made not
to cheat. I'm proud of you for that."

Turn to page 44.

"Ms. Shelton, I would like some help," you reply.

"All right, then I'll meet you here after school on Tuesdays and Wednesdays, and I'll expect you to stay in during recess for extra help," Ms. Shelton says.

The thought of missing recess really bugs you, but if it means getting good enough grades so your parents will let you keep playing soccer, you'll do just about anything.

That night at home you turn over your report card to your parents with a note from Ms. Shelton explaining how you're going to be working with her. Your parents accept the plan and offer their help.

For the next month, you work closely with Ms. Shelton. It's really hard when you look out the window at recess and see all the other kids, including Karen, having fun and playing games. It seems like you haven't seen Karen at all.

Turn to page 45.

You wish that Ms. Shelton had asked you to work hard at soccer or basketball or even gym class instead. Working hard at spelling and math isn't much fun. But you nod your head yes anyway.

"Good, then," she states, "I'll see you after school Tuesdays and Thursdays for extra help. We'll check homework and do some studying. I'll team you up with Ashley and Rebecca. They stay after school and help with classroom chores. They can help you, too."

The idea sounds okay, and for about a week you stay after. But then you get involved with extra soccer practice with your friends after school and you miss some sessions. When you miss the second time, Ms. Shelton calls home.

Your mom is waiting for you when you get home.

"Jen, I can understand having a hard time at school. But I don't understand not showing us your report card," she said, frowning.

Your parents make you spend a lot of time at home and in Ms. Shelton's room working on math and social studies for the rest of the term.

Basketball season comes and goes without you. The schoolwork is hard, but you keep trying. At the end of the second term, your report card shows two B's, a B-, and two C's. You know what hard work means, in school as well as in sports.

The End

"No way, Dan! They'll make me quit soccer," you say firmly. "I just can't show them. Not now!"
You don't want to work with Dan either; you think he might want you to leave soccer practice early.

"Maybe you can help me later on. I'll figure this out," you say.

The soccer tournament turns out great that weekend. Your team, the Lions, beats the Strikers three to one! You win first place.

But Tuesday of the next week, your dad comes home and asks about your report card. There's no way out of it. You turn it over, and he is really upset.

"I don't believe this!" he says loudly. "I can see you've been burning the candle at both ends, young lady. I'm going to talk to your teacher tomorrow."

The next day you wait outside the room trying to hear what Ms. Shelton says to your parents. The door opens.

"Come in, Jennifer," Ms. Shelton says.

"Jennifer, we have decided you need to cut out sports this winter," your dad explains. "Ms. Shelton has agreed to help you after school a couple of days a week."

For two months you do everything your parents and Ms. Shelton ask. You work really hard.

Your next report card shows one A, two B's, and one B-. It's *much* better. You realize that it's not easy to be an athlete and a good student at the same time.

The End

Ms. Shelton hands out the second term report card in January. She's smiling—it's is a good sign. Your heart feels like a basketball bouncing on the court. You sit back in your seat and open it slowly.

There, in big, black letters, are three B's and two C's. You turn to Karen and give her a high five.

"Ladies, please," Ms. Shelton calls out, but you can see that she is still smiling.

You whisper across the aisle to Karen, "Thanks for helping me out."

The End

You decide to try the study skills course. Two days later you are sitting in the Learning Center working on drills, learning about organization, and learning how to keep a notebook properly. Actually, you don't mind the help.

For the next two months you go there three times a week. You learn how to outline, how to read for detail, how to find the main point, and a lot of other important ideas. At school, you use some of the things they teach you.

Where it really shows is in your grades. Slowly, you are doing better. Your confidence grows.

At the end of the next term, you bring your report card straight home. No F's and no D's.

"We are so proud of your improvement," your mom says, smiling.

You feel great!

The End

You really don't want to go to a study skills course, so you ask your mom and dad to give you one more chance. They say okay, but you have to work out a plan with them.

Each day at school you have to write down your homework in an assignment book for them to see. They want you to clean out your desk at school and your room at home.

The plan includes no TV on weekdays.

"But I'll miss cartoons!" you protest.

"Jennifer, you'll miss passing fourth grade if you don't do better," your dad says.

Amazingly, they let you continue to play soccer. You are very glad since that weekend your team plays for the tournament championship.

Each night you work real hard on your homework and studying. At least half the time either Mom or Dad sits with you coaching, helping, and studying. It feels good to know that they are there to help you when you need it.

By the end of the second term, you know that you are doing better. When the report card comes out, you have improved in three subjects. Ms. Shelton gives you an award for Most Improved Student in social studies and math!

Karen calls over, "Hey, Most Improved Jennifer, what's two plus two?"

You both laugh. You are pleased when you take your report card home that night, and so are your parents!

The End

"Dan, I am trying!" you say to him.

"Jen, you can't pull that on me. I tried it all myself once. Look at it this way, when you had trouble last season with corner kicks, what did you do?" he asks.

"I practiced and practiced until I learned it," you answer. "I'm pretty good at them now."

"Well, schoolwork is just like that," he says.

You think about that for a long time and you finally understand.

You and Dan tell your parents about your bad report card and your new plan. They agree to let you work with Dan.

For the next two months you work really hard, just like it was soccer practice. When it gets more difficult, you try even harder.

Dan makes it fun sometimes. He makes up games for studying spelling words. When you do real well, you both go out and kick the soccer ball around for a break. He's really proud of the way you are working. You feel good about that.

At the end of the term you run straight to Dan with your report card. It shows three B's and two C's. He gives you a big hug.

"I guess you won that game," he says.

All you can do is smile!

The End

You understand what Dan means, but it is just too hard to put the effort in.

First, you have soccer practice and the upcoming tournament. Then there are your friends to see, especially Karen. With Thanksgiving and then Christmas coming up, there's just too much on your mind.

Dan helps when you ask him, but you only do that three or four times.

Your parents find out about the report card.

"That's the end of your fourth grade vacation, Jennifer." your dad says angrily. They tell you that you can't watch TV anymore or have any friends over until the grades go up.

"No cartoons? No *Disney*?" you ask.

"No TV at all," your mom answers.

This term seems like a very long time. You are even more worried about next term.

The End

41   You really don't plan on cheating, but it was so easy last time that when the math test begins, you start thinking about it again. Josh's paper is uncovered on his desk. It's really not too hard to peek at his paper. You get a few answers from him.

As you line up for lunch, Ms. Shelton says, "Jennifer Warner, please remain here for a minute." Your heart drops into your stomach— exactly where your lunch is supposed to go.

When she returns after taking the other kids to lunch she looks you straight in the eye.

"Jennifer, I know you cheated on the math test today, and I know you're having trouble in school. I'm going to give you a choice. I can either tell your parents about the cheating, or you'll have to deal with me. It won't be fun, either way," she says.

If you decide to deal with Ms. Shelton,
turn to page 48.

If you decide to let her tell your parents,
turn to page 49.

Your parents work hard with you that entire **44** term. You find out that your dad knows quite a lot about math, and your mom is good at science and spelling. You sort of knew that before, but now that you need help, it really sinks in.

You get some good quiz grades, and you are really proud of them. One thing leads to another, and you start doing better in most of your subjects. On one math test you get a score of 96!

By the end of the term, your report card shows a great improvement.

Your mom gives you another big hug.

"Like I told you two months ago," she says, "I am really proud of you."

The End

45   One day, after Ms. Shelton has been working with you for a few weeks, she says, "Jennifer, I'm going to give your parents a call. It seems to me that you have a slight problem with reading and writing that I didn't notice before. You know how sometimes you have some trouble reading certain types of words and writing long passages from the book?"

You nod your head.

"Well, I'll see if your parents would like you to meet with Mrs. Simmons, our school psychologist. She would give you some special tests that might tell us about how you learn. She could also tell us if there is anything special we should look for."

"Do you think I'm dumb, Ms. Shelton?" you ask worriedly.

"No, Jennifer, not at all," she smiles. "Most kids who have learning problems are actually very smart."

You're not sure if you want to see Mrs. Simmons, or not.

If you and your parents want you to see Mrs. Simmons, turn to page 52.

If you don't want to see Mrs. Simmons, turn to page 54.

Ms. Shelton was right; it's not fun. For the first two weeks, all you do is clean boards, copy notes, put papers in alphabetical order, and all sorts of other chores.

"I wish I'd never looked at Josh's paper in the first place," you mutter to yourself.

But then, as time goes on, you begin to do schoolwork with Ms. Shelton. Once you get to know her, you realize that she can be pretty funny and nice.

Your parents soon find out about the report card. Ms. Shelton talks to them on the phone, and they agree to let you work with her, but they don't let you try out for basketball.

At the end of the term, your report card is much improved. You have one A, three B's, and one C. You feel excited and proud, just like when you score the winning goal in a soccer game. Your parents are happy too.

And, of course, you give up cheating.

The End

49   You feel like things can't get any worse, and you don't know what to do about it.

"I don't care," you say, discouraged. "You can tell them."

When you go home that evening, you expect them to jump all over you. Your stomach is so tight and knotted up that you think you might get sick. You take a deep breath and open the front door.

You're surprised when your parents calmly ask you to sit down and talk.

"Jen," your dad says, "we know you've been super busy this school year. Your mom and I think maybe you've been doing too much. I'm sure that's part of the reason why you're not doing well and also why you cheated on the test.

"You can stay on the soccer team, but there will be no more TV—period. We want you to concentrate on your schoolwork. And no more cheating."

"Absolutely, Dad," you say, "and I'm really sorry."

Turn to page 60.

You decide to see Mrs. Simmons. Your parents say it's okay. She is friendly and fun, and after getting to know her, you take some different kinds of tests.

Some are like regular school tests with paper and pencil. Some have blocks and designs. Some are almost like games. When she explains that they will help give your teachers an idea of how you learn and how to help you, you don't mind at all.

When the tests are all done, Mrs. Simmons meets with your mom and dad. You wait outside for awhile, and then they invite you in for a meeting.

She explains that you have above-average intelligence but just a slight learning problem. It probably was not picked up before because you are smart and learned to work around it. When the work got harder, your learning problem showed up.

"You mean I'm not dumb?" you ask quietly.

"Far from it," Mrs. Simmons says.

She recommends that you go to the Resource Room three times a week for extra help from the special education teacher.

It sounds okay to you.

Turn to page 56.

53

You aren't excited about seeing Mrs. Simmons.
When you talk to your parents about it, they say it's up to you.

"You can improve your grades yourself if you really work at it," they say.

So you continue to work with Ms. Shelton. Your grades improve a bit, but it is still pretty hard for you. As long as you put in a lot of effort, you get some good results. But as soon as you forget to study or don't work hard, your grades go down again.

"Skimble," you say to your cat one night, "why can't this be as easy as a penalty kick?"

All term you keep at it. By the end you have done better in a few subjects. You have two B's, two C's and one D on your report card. It's an improvement.

You realize that in order to do well, you really have to do your homework every day.

"Being a student isn't easy," you tell Skimble. "It's even harder than being an athlete."

The End

Going to the Resource Room helps a lot. The
teachers there seem to know exactly how to help.

One teacher shows you how to scan what you're
reading to pick out the important points. Another
time they explain how to proofread your own
writing so you can make your own corrections.

When you have a problem with a certain bit of
homework, they know a better way to do the work.
They tell you how to organize your work and your
notebooks. You follow their directions and things
start getting easier at school.

You still work with Ms. Shelton. With all the
help, plus the effort that you are putting in, your
grades improve.

Your parents are happy, and you can't wait until
spring soccer camp!

The End

COMMUNITY BILLBOARD

INFORMATION

SOCCER

WORLD CUP

PELE

SOCCER BASICS

SOCCER
BASICS

You decide there is no way that you are going to **58**
cheat again. Never mind the fact that you might
get caught; it just isn't right. Besides, you can't
stand those butterflies in your stomach or your
hands sweating when you think about it.

From that day on, you really try harder in school.
You study and work on weekends. You ask Karen
for help, and she doesn't mind. Of course, your
parents soon find out about the report card. They
are upset but they agree to give you a chance to
improve your grades.

Amazingly, things get better. Your test and quiz
scores improve. You even get a score of 96 on a
science test!

Ms. Shelton smiles at you when she hands the
test back to you, "Well, who is this new scientist we
have in class? Congratulations, Jennifer!"

You know that you've found a good way to handle
your schoolwork.

The End

REPORT CARD

A		B	
B		A	
B+		A	
A-		C	
B		B	

You can do it, too —

Sincerely,

Jen.

You decide to change your ways. Your mom and dad help, and you begin to get organized. Every day you do your homework first thing after soccer practice. You start your long term reports and book reports way ahead of time, and they turn out pretty good. You study for tests with your parents, one of your brothers, or even Karen.

It's not easy, and you have to work hard all term long. Finally, even your test scores start to improve.

You feel better about your schoolwork, and you appreciate the fact that your parents gave you a second chance.

It proves to be worth it. Your second report card is much improved, and your soccer team is doing great! In the final tournament game, you score two goals to help your team win the championship!

The End

The Decision Is Yours Series

These are fun books that help children ages 7-11 think about social problems. Written in the "choose-your-own-ending" format, the child gets to decide what action the character will take and then gets to see the consequences.

Finders, Keepers?
By Elizabeth Crary
What do you do when your friend wants to take money from a wallet you found and buy ice cream?

Bully on the Bus
By Carl Bosch
What do you do when Nick, a big kid in the fifth grade, wants to beat you up?

Making the Grade
By Carl Bosch
Help Jennifer decide what to do about a bad report card after she spends more time on the soccer field than with her homework.

$3.95 each, paper, 64 pages, illus.

Biographies for Young Children

These books tell the stories of spunky girls in history who grew up to make significant changes in our society. These picture-story books are fun and riveting for preschoolers and simple enough for an eight year old to read alone.

Elizabeth Blackwell—the story of the first woman doctor.

Harriet Tubman—the story of the famous conductor on the Underground Railroad.

Juliette Gordon Low—the story of the founder of the Girl Scouts.

$5.95 each, paperback, 32 pages, illus.

ORDER FORM

Finders, Keepers	$3.95 ___		Elizabeth Blackwell	$5.95 ___
Bully on the Bus	$3.95 ___		Harriet Tubman	$5.95 ___
Making the Grade	$3.95 ___		Juliette Gordon Low	$5.95 ___

Subtotal _____

Shipping _____

Tax (WA add 8.2%) _____

Total _____

Name _____

Address _____

City _____

State/zip _____

Order subtotal	Shipping
$ 0-$10	add 2.95
$10-$25	add 3.95
$25-$50	add 4.95

Send to: Parenting Press, Inc; P.O.Box 75267, Dept.103; Seattle, WA 98125, or phone: 1-800-992-6657